The Friendly Fox

To Ella Baruch
JK

To the fox
BG

The Friendly Fox

JENNY KORALEK

ILLUSTRATED BY BEVERLEY GOODING

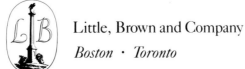

Little, Brown and Company

Boston · Toronto

First U.S. edition

Library of Congress Cataloging-in-Publication Data

Koralek, Jenny.
    The friendly fox / Jenny Koralek : illustrated by Beverley
Gooding. — 1st U.S. ed.
        p. cm.
    Summary: Relates how a friendly fox wins the confidence of the
animals that are afraid of him.
    ISBN 0-316-50179-4 (lib. bdg.)
    [1. Foxes — Fiction. 2. Friendship — Fiction. 3. Animals —
Fiction.] I. Gooding, Beverley, ill. II. Title.
PZ.K8363Fr 1988
[E] — dc19

10 9 8 7 6 5 4 3 2 1

First published in Great Britain in 1988 by Methuen
Children's Books Ltd.

Printed in Hong Kong by South China Printing Co

The illustrations were executed in Caran D'Ache crayon
and watercolor.

Once upon a time there was a lonely fox
who lived in a wood far away over the hills.

He chased rabbits but he never caught one.

He chased the chickens in the farmyard,
but he never caught one.

He was quite happy to eat turnips and fallen apples.

"Why do I chase rabbits and chickens?"
he asked the old owl in the oak tree.
    "You chase them," said the owl, "because
that is what foxes are supposed to do.
But I have heard tell that behind the sun
and beyond the moon there is a far land
where the lion lies down with the lamb,
dogs and cats play together all the livelong
day and foxes are friends with the rabbits . . ."
    "And with the chickens?" asked the fox.

"And with the chickens," said the owl.
    "How I wish I lived there," sighed the fox.

The next day, when the rabbits came out to
play again, the fox ran across the field
to talk to them, but they all hopped away.

Then he tried to make friends with the chickens,
but every time he went down to the farmyard
the rooster crowed, the mother hen clucked
and all the little chickens hid from him.

What is more, the farmer's wife flapped
her big apron at him. The farmer tried
to shoot him with his gun and then the
huntsmen came after him on huge horses.
The poor fox had to run for his life.
He was very sad.

"Why do the rabbits run away from me?"
he asked the owl.

"Why are the chickens afraid of me?
Why did the farmer try to shoot me and
the huntsmen try to kill me?"

"Because you are a fox," said the owl.
"You are an enemy. They think you will
eat the rabbits and the chickens."

"Me? Eat the rabbits and the chickens?"
said the fox. "But I only want to play with them."

"Then you must make friends with them,"
said the owl, "and go with them to the
far land behind the sun and beyond the moon.
If you stay here you will always
be hunted, and once the rabbits
and the chickens are big and fat,
the farmer's wife will turn them
into hot roast dinners."

The fox shivered and shook.
"What shall I do?"
he cried. "Oh, what
shall I do?"

"Wish on the first star every night till
summer comes," said the owl, "and you
will see what you will see."

So every night the fox wished on the
first star that he could make friends
with the rabbits and the chickens and go
with them to the far land.

One day the farmer's wife left the door
of the chicken-run open. The rooster
was taking a dust-bath.

The mother hen was in the nesting box
keeping a new egg warm.

So all the little chickens ran away.
They were bored in the chicken-run all day
long, scratching and pecking at the corn.
They went into the big green field.

"Hello," they said to the rabbits. "Will you
play with us?"

"Play what?" said the rabbits.

"Chicken Whispers," said the chickens.

"Chicken Whispers?" said the rabbits.
And they rolled about laughing.

"Chicken Whispers!"

So the chickens turned up their beaks
and went on into the woods.

They had fun for a while flying
into the trees

or pecking at the wild strawberries.

When they were tired they sat in a circle
and played Chicken Whispers by themselves.

Suddenly they heard a growly voice say,
"Can I play too?" It was the fox. The chickens
squawked and clucked and ran around
trying to find the right path home. But the
fox said, "I won't hurt you, really, I won't.
I only want to play."

So the chickens made a place for him
in the circle and they played
Chicken Whispers and Chicken of
the Castle and Fox's Bluff.

That was the best game. One chicken sat on the fox's head and covered the fox's eyes with his wings and the fox pretended to catch the little chickens. They made so much noise the rabbits crept up to watch.

When they were all tired of games the fox
said, "Sit down and I'll tell you a story."
And he told them about the far land behind the
sun and beyond the moon where all the
animals are friends.

    "Let's go there," said the chickens.
    "Let's go there now."
    "Can we come too?" said the rabbits.
    "Yes," said the fox. "We will all go there.
But not yet. Go home and wait till
the leaves fall to the ground."

And when all the leaves had fallen to the
ground the fox sent the rabbits to dig a
big hole under the chicken-run.

"Is it time?" whispered the chickens.
"Is it time now to go to the far land?"

"Not yet," whispered the rabbits. "Fox
is waiting till the snow comes when everybody
stays indoors by the fire and you cannot hear
a single footstep. Then we'll go. Isn't it
a good secret? Oh, isn't it a good secret?"

The farmer and his wife never saw the
big hole hidden under the leaves.
  "Our chickens have grown so big and fat,"
said the farmer to his wife. "What lovely
roast dinners they will make!"
  And the chickens laughed quietly because
they had such a good secret.

One night the frost came. There was ice
in all the puddles and the snow began to fall.
As soon as it was dark, and when everybody
was indoors by the fire, the fox came
silently over the thick, soft snow.

He lay down and let the chickens climb onto his warm back and the rabbits followed behind in a line. And just as the moon was rising they set out for the far land where all the animals are friends and they were never seen again.

Of course, the farmer and his wife were
quite sure the fox had eaten the chickens
and the rabbits. But the old owl in the
oak tree knew where they had gone and now
you know too, don't you?